Author:

Alex Woolf studied history at Essex University, England. He is the author of over 60 books for children, including *You Wouldn't Want to Live Without Bees!*, *You Wouldn't Want to Live Without Vegetables!*, and *The Science of Acne and Warts: The Itchy Truth About Skin*.

Series creator:

David Salariya was born in Dundee, Scotland. He has illustrated a wide range of books and has created and designed many new series for publishers in the UK and overseas. David established The Salariya Book Company in 1989. He lives in Brighton with his wife, illustrator Shirley Willis, and their son Jonathan.

Artists:

Bryan Beach
David Pavon
Caroline Romanet
Andy Rowland
Paco Sordo
Diego Vaisberg

Editor:

Jacqueline Ford

Published in Great Britain in MMXVIII by
Book House, an imprint of
The Salariya Book Company Ltd
25 Marlborough Place, Brighton BN1 1UB
www.salariya.com

HB ISBN: 978-1-912006-12-0
PB ISBN: 978-1-912006-40-3

SALARIYA
SCRIBO BOOK HOUSE SCRIBBLERS

1 3 5 7 9 8 6 4 2

A CIP catalogue record for this book is available from the British Library.

Printed and bound in China.

Visit
www.salariya.com
for our online catalogue and
free fun stuff.

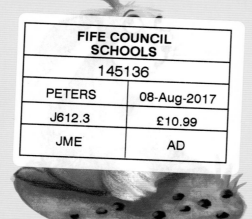

The Science of Poo and Farts

The Smelly Truth About Digestion

Written by
Alex Woolf

BOOK HOUSE
a SALARIYA *imprint*

Contents

Introduction

We all do it. Boys and girls, teachers and firefighters, doctors and astronauts, kings and queens – everyone poos. It may seem pretty gross, but it's perfectly healthy and natural. Poo (also called faeces or excrement) is the solid waste that's left after we've digested our food. It's the stuff our bodies can't use for energy or growth, and it passes out of us when we go to the toilet. So poo is really just the final product of our digestive system.

In this book we will explore how we digest our food, and all the strange side effects of this complex and fascinating process – including burps and farts. We will look at what happens when things go wrong, and how this affects the colour, smell and texture of our poo. We will also find out how poo is not just a smelly waste product, but can actually be useful to us.

Along the way, you will discover all sorts of fascinating facts and disgusting data, including some of the revolting things animals do with their poo!

How do we produce poo?

Mouth and oesophagus

In digestion, the breaking-down process of food begins in your mouth. Your teeth crush food into small, soft pieces. Saliva makes food moist and easy to swallow. When you swallow, the food goes down a tube called the oesophagus and into the stomach.

The story of how we produce poo starts with the food we eat. Our bodies break down the food into useful substances that enable us to be active, to grow and to stay healthy. This breaking-down process is called digestion, and it happens in the digestive system. The digestive system is like a long tube, nearly 9 metres (29.5 ft) in length, that starts at the mouth and ends at the anus. It is made up of several different organs, each of which helps in the process of turning food into useful substances. At the end of the process, when there are no more useful substances left, whatever is left leaves the body as poo.

Have a good journey!

Tongue

Salivary glands

Oesophagus

Stomach

Poo is made up of around 75 percent water and 25 percent solid matter. The solid matter is made up of undigestible fibre, living and dead bacteria (germs), cells and mucus.

Fascinating fact

Food doesn't need gravity to get to your stomach. Muscles in your oesophagus push the food down, so you could eat while standing on your head.

Stomach

When food enters the stomach, the muscles of the stomach wall churn the food around. Gastric juices mix with the food, breaking it down further. The food is turned into a thick liquid called chyme.

Intestines

The chyme is squirted into the small intestine, where digestive juices break it down into nutrients that are carried away to other parts of the body. The remaining waste passes to the large intestine, or colon. The colon walls absorb water from the waste, making it dry and solid (poo). The poo is stored in the rectum until you go to the toilet.

Large intestine

Small intestine

Stomach

Rectum

It takes between 30 and 50 hours for food to travel from mouth to anus.

Oesophagus

Stomach

Small intestine

How do kidneys work?

Inside each kidney are millions of tiny tubes called nephrons. As blood travels around the nephrons, waste (some water, salts, minerals and other chemicals) is filtered out. The waste is collected at the centre of the kidneys, where it is turned into urine.

Blood, waste and water enter through this artery

Cleaned blood leaves through this vein

Urine leaves through the ureter

If the kidneys didn't clean the blood, the waste would build up in the body and make us sick.

What is wee?

The body produces wee, or urine, as another way of getting rid of waste. Waste is produced when the body digests food and turns it into energy. This collects in the blood. The waste is taken out of the blood by bean-shaped organs called kidneys. You have two kidneys, one on either side of your spine. The kidneys filter the waste out of the blood, then send the cleaned blood back around the body. The kidneys also remove excess water from the blood. They turn the waste and water into urine, which then goes to the bladder, where it is stored until you need to go to the toilet.

Some ancient Romans rinsed their mouths out with wee for whiter teeth. Yuck!

Wee gets its yellow colour from a chemical called bilirubin, produced by the liver. The kidneys remove bilirubin from the blood, so it ends up in your urine.

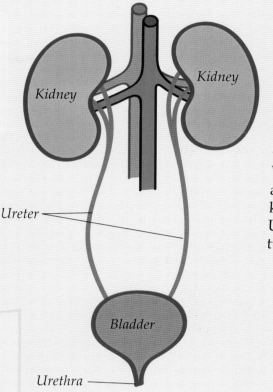

Kidney

Kidney

Ureter

Bladder

Urethra

How does urine leave the body?

The urine leaves the kidneys via a tube called a ureter, which takes it to the bladder. The bladder is a stretchy bag that slowly fills up with urine. When it's nearly full, it sends a signal to your brain and you know it's time to do a wee. Urine leaves your body via a tube called the urethra.

Dialysis

You can survive perfectly well with just one kidney, but you would be very ill if both kidneys stopped working properly. People whose kidneys do not work properly can have their blood cleaned by a dialysis machine.

Can you believe it?

The average adult produces 1.5 litres (6.3 cups) of urine a day. By contrast, an elephant produces nearly 50 litres (208 cups)!

9

Tree shrew toilets

The tropical pitcher plant has tube-shaped leaves that are used as toilets by the tree shrew. After the shrew has done its business, the poo it has left provides the plant with lots of nutrition.

Animal poo

Just like humans, animals have to get rid of waste in the form of poo. Animal poo is often called dung, scat, manure or droppings. Animals use their own poo, and the poo of other animals, in all sorts of strange and inventive ways. For example, big cats, wolves, monkeys and wombats use their urine and poo to mark out their territory and warn other animals away. Wombats even manage to produce cube-shaped poos, so they don't roll away. The potato beetle larva uses its poo for protection. It covers itself in its own poisonous faeces as a defence against predators.

Hippos spin their tails to launch their poo underwater.

Are you sure you want to do this?

Can you believe it?

Termites grow fungus gardens inside their mounds as a source of food. They fertilise the fungus with their own droppings.

Dung beetles use the dung of larger animals as a source of food and shelter, while the larvae of some leaf beetles make homes out of their own dung.

Bird-dung crab spider

To protect itself from predators, the bird-dung crab spider disguises itself as – you've guessed it – bird poo! When it draws its legs in and sits very still, it mimics bird droppings in colour, shape and even smell!

Disgusting data

Rabbits sometimes produce a soft poo called cecotropes, which is so nutritious, they eat it!

11

The average person farts, on average, 14 times a day, producing about half a litre of gas.

What are farts?

They can make quite a noise, and they can smell terrible! You might get embarrassed if you do one in public. But don't worry – everyone farts. Farting, or passing wind, is just a natural by-product of digestion. Farts are gas released by the body. The gas comes from several different sources. Some of it is air we have swallowed while eating. Some is gas that seeps into our intestines from our blood, and some is gas produced by the digestive process and by bacteria living in our guts. These gases can't stay in the body, so they come out as farts!

Why do farts stink?

A typical fart mostly contains non-smelly gases such as nitrogen, hydrogen, carbon dioxide and oxygen. The bad smell comes from gases containing sulphur, such as hydrogen sulphide, which make up just one percent of an average fart. If you eat lots of foods that contain sulphur (see below), you're more likely to produce really smelly farts.

Fizzy drinks

Cabbage

Beans

Eggs

Cheese

Why do farts make that noise?

We all know that sound. You can imitate it by blowing a raspberry. Farts make this sound when they come out by causing vibrations in the rectum. The loudness of the noise varies depending on the pressure of the gas as it escapes and the tightness of the muscles in the anus.

Can you believe it?

The larvae of the beaded lacewing live in termite nests, and when they get hungry they stun the termites with their farts, then eat them. One fart is powerful enough to immobilize six termites!

Is it an earthquake?

No, I think it's the beans!

Beware the lacewing fart. It's silent, but deadly!

Farts can travel at up to 3 metres per second. Most are slower, taking 10 to 15 seconds to reach another person's nostrils.

Do some foods make you fart more?

Certain foods, like beans, onions and fried foods, release larger amounts of gas as they break down in your body. Some people have a hard time digesting foods containing lactose, a sugar found in dairy foods, and this can cause them to fart more than the usual amount.

Fizzy drinks

Fizzy drinks can bring on big burps. Why? Because they contain bubbles of a gas called carbon dioxide. Other causes of burping are drinking through a straw and eating or drinking too quickly.

The sound of a burp is caused by the escaping gas making a flap of tissue at the top of the oesophagus vibrate.

What are burps?

Have you ever accidentally made a loud burp during a meal? While you're apologising to the other diners, you may be wondering where that came from. A burp is made of gas. When you eat, you don't only swallow food and drink, you also swallow air. Air contains gases like nitrogen and oxygen. These gases end up in your stomach. When there's too much gas in the stomach, it's forced up through the oesophagus and out of the mouth as a burp. And it comes out very quickly, which is why you can't always cover your mouth in time.

Too much food?

No, too much air.

Burping babies

When babies feed, they collect a lot of gas in their stomachs. Because they find it hard to burp on their own, this builds up and can cause them discomfort. That's why babies need to be 'burped', or patted on the back, to help them release the gas.

Well done!

You're never that happy when I burp.

Birds don't burp. But fish do – through their gills.

Cow burps

Pardon me!

Cows burp a gas called methane, which contributes to global warming. Every year, cows in the U.S. burp about 50 million tonnes of methane. The burps of ten cows could emit enough of this gas to keep a small house heated for a year.

Fascinating fact

In some breeds of dog, such as Great Danes and Irish setters, a failure to burp can be fatal. In a condition called 'bloat', gas gets trapped in their stomachs. A flexible rubber tube is inserted down the dog's throat to expel the gas.

What is saliva?

As well as helping to break down food, the enzymes in saliva also fight off infections in the mouth and teeth.

Salivary glands

Saliva is produced by salivary glands, which are found on the inside of each cheek and on the bottom of the mouth.

It's not very pleasant when someone spits in public, or if you see a long string of drool dangling from a person's mouth. Yet spit, or saliva – the frothy liquid we produce in our mouths – plays a very important role in the body. It keeps your mouth moist; it makes food wet and slippery, so it's easier to swallow; it helps your tongue taste things; and it starts the process of digestion. Saliva contains chemicals called enzymes, which start to break down food, even before it reaches the stomach. Some animals use saliva in interesting ways. Llamas, for example, will spit at other animals if they feel threatened. They can spit up to 3 metres (10 ft).

Salivary glands

16

How dare you take my photo!

Dry mouth

When you are nervous or frightened, you produce less saliva, making your mouth feel dry. Other causes of dry mouth are hot weather, drinking too little water, and heavy exercise.

The spitting spider produces a substance containing venom and a sticky kind of silk. It spits this at its prey, paralysing it. The spider can then eat its victim at its leisure.

The average person produces just under a litre of saliva a day – enough to fill two bathtubs a year.

Swift saliva

Some species of swift use their saliva to build their nests. The saliva hardens to a glue that holds the nest together. This sticky saliva is used to make the Chinese delicacy, bird's nest soup.

What are diarrhoea and vomiting?

What causes diarrhoea?

Diarrhoea is caused by germs such as viruses and bacteria. These can get into your body via contaminated food or drink, or through contact with an infected person or animal.

To avoid the germs that cause diarrhoea, always wash your hands with soap after going to the toilet and before you prepare or eat any food.

Sometimes you might get a pain in your stomach and an urgent need to go to the toilet. When you go, your poo is runny or watery. This is diarrhoea. It happens because you have eaten some food that your body needs to get rid of quickly. The food may have gone bad or perhaps it contains something poisonous or something to which you are allergic. Normally it takes between 6 and 15 hours for food to pass through the intestines. In these cases, the food is rushed through your intestines much faster than normal. There isn't enough time for the water in it to be absorbed, which is why the poo, when it comes out, is soft and runny.

Emergency! Get out of the way!

Toilet

Vomiting

Urrrggghh! Sometimes your body has to get rid of bad or poisonous food before it even reaches the intestines – when it's still in the stomach. Vomiting is a powerful, violent urge that you just can't stop, often leading to a mess on the floor.

What happens when you vomit?

When you vomit, a ring of muscle at the top of the stomach relaxes, and stomach muscles force the food into the oesophagus and then up and out through the mouth. The vomit tastes horrible because the food has been mixed with the acidic juices in your stomach.

The fulmar is a sea bird. When another bird tries to eat a fulmar chick, the chick will vomit a slimy substance that sticks to the predator's feathers.

Helpful hint

Diarrhoea makes you lose fluids and can cause dehydration. If you get diarrhoea, make sure you drink plenty of water. Sports drinks and special rehydration drinks can also help.

What is constipation?

Constipation has many causes, including a lack of fibre in your diet, insufficient exercise and anxiety. Even a change of routine, like going on holiday, can cause constipation.

Sometimes you feel like you want to poo, but you can't. Or doing it might be difficult and need a lot more pushing than normal. When it comes out, the faeces is often small, hard and lumpy. You might have a feeling that not everything came out. These are all signs of constipation. Almost everyone gets constipated at some point in their lives, and it's usually not serious. Constipation is the opposite of diarrhoea – food stays in the intestines for longer than normal, so more water is absorbed, making the poo dry and hard.

Toilet terrors

When people feel stressed, for example before an exam, they might become constipated. A fear of public toilets can cause some people to suppress the urge to poo.

Poo chart

The Bristol stool chart was developed to show the different kinds of poo. Poo varies in shape and texture depending on how long it takes food to pass through your intestines. This chart can help doctors diagnose digestive problems.

 Type 1: Separate hard lumps – very constipated

 Type 2: Lumpy and sausage like – slightly constipated

 Type 3: Sausage-like with cracks in the surface – normal

 Type 4: A smooth, soft sausage or snake – normal

 Type 5: Soft blobs with clear-cut edges – normal

 Type 6: Mushy with ragged edges – diarrhoea

 Type 7: Liquid with no solid pieces – diarrhoea

Fabulous fibre

One cause of constipation is not eating enough fibre. Fibre is found in fruits, vegetables and wholegrain cereals. It is bulky and helps food move easily through the intestines.

Call a doctor if you see blood in your stool, if you have severe pain when you poo, or if your constipation has lasted for more than two weeks.

Helpful hint

If you are constipated:
- drink lots of water
- eat more fruit and veg
- eat prunes and bran cereal

Digestive problems

What is heartburn?

Heartburn, or acid reflux, happens when stomach acid escapes into the oesophagus. Because the oesophagus is not as well protected as the stomach, this can produce a burning sensation in the chest and throat.

You're breathing fire!

It may just be heartburn.

Why doesn't stomach acid damage your stomach? Because the stomach's lining is coated with mucus, which protects it from the acid.

Most of the time, if your digestive system is working properly, you should feel no discomfort at all after eating a meal. Sometimes, however, things can go wrong. Perhaps you feel uncomfortably full or bloated, or suffer a burning sensation above your stomach (heartburn). You may feel sick. You may burp a lot, or even vomit. These are all signs of indigestion. Causes can include eating greasy or spicy foods, eating too much, eating too quickly, exercising too soon after eating, or stress.

Eaten too much again?

What are food allergies?

Sometimes the body's immune system (which provides resistance to infection) reacts to particular foods. It might cause itching or swelling inside the mouth or throat, an itchy red rash, swelling of the face, or vomiting. This is an allergic reaction. Here are some foods that commonly cause allergic reactions:

Milk

Peanuts

Fish

Shellfish

Eggs

Up to 1 in 12 children have a food allergy, and 40% of them have a severe reaction. The good news is, many children outgrow their allergies.

What is a hiccup?

A hiccup is a quick, involuntary intake of air. It happens when a muscle called the diaphragm contracts sharply. Hiccups can happen if you irritate your stomach by eating too much food. The 'hick!' sound is caused by the sudden closure of your vocal chords.

Hiccup 'cures'

Sip ice-cold water

Hold your breath

Bite on a lemon

Can you believe it?

The longest bout of hiccups lasted 68 years. Charles Osborne (1894–1991) suffered non-stop hiccups from 1922 to 1990.

HICCUP!

HICCUP!

A healthy diet

If you become very overweight, it can be bad for your health. So to stay healthy, we should limit our intake of foods that are high in sugar and carbohydrates.

Your diet is everything you eat and drink. A healthy diet (also called a balanced diet) provides you with all the nutrients you need. There are four main groups of nutrients: proteins (found in meat, fish, eggs and nuts); vitamins and minerals (fresh fruit and vegetables); carbohydrates (potatoes, rice, bread and sugary foods); and fats (fried foods, dairy products and nuts). Many people are attracted to foods that are high in carbohydrates and fats, such as fried and sugary foods, because they find them delicious. If you eat too much of these high-energy foods, your body will store the extra calories as fat.

Proteins

Proteins are the building blocks of the body. They help your body grow strong and repair damage such as cuts, bruises and broken bones. For vegetarians and vegans, nuts, lentils and chickpeas are good sources of protein.

Will steak make my leg better?

It's a balanced meal.

It needs to be balanced with a serious amount of cake!

24

Most doctors think we should try to eat at least five portions of fresh fruit and vegetables a day.

Carbohydrates and fats

Carbohydrates are the most important source of energy for your body. There are two main kinds: starch (found in potatoes, rice and bread) and sugars (found in fruit, vegetables, milk and dairy products). Fats also provide us with energy, as well as other important chemicals that our bodies need.

Starchy foods give you a steady amount of energy.

Sugary foods give you quick bursts of energy!

Vitamins and minerals

Your body only needs tiny amounts of vitamins and minerals, but they are essential for keeping you fit and healthy.

Oranges contain vitamin C, which will help my body fight off colds.

Fascinating fact

Energy in food is called calories. By exercising, you can burn off calories. It would take more than an hour of walking to burn off all the calories in a slice of cake with icing.

Can poo be useful?

Animal dung has been used as a building material or to make paper and gunpowder. Conservationists examine dung to learn about the health and whereabouts of animals.

Faeces fertiliser

Farmers have been using animal poo as a fertiliser for thousands of years. They use dung from horses, cattle, sheep, pigs and chickens, as well as guano from bats and birds. Even panda poo has been used to fertilise tea plants in China.

Hmm – a faint smell of pandas.

We usually think of poo as a waste product – something to get rid of in the toilet. Yet it can be a surprisingly useful substance. For example, farmers use animal dung, or manure, to fertilise their crops. The manure contains lots of nutrients that make the soil more fertile. Poo is also a source of energy. It can be converted into biogas, which can provide heat and electricity. Biogas can be turned into biomethane to power cars. And archaeologists study ancient poo to learn about the diet and lifestyle of our early ancestors.

At least it doesn't smell anymore.

Samples of Ancient Poo

Poo power

The gas from animal poo is warmed in airtight containers. Bacteria then turns the poo into a fuel called biogas, which can be burned to generate heat and power. The poo of 500 cows can create enough electricity to power 100 homes.

Poo → *Anaerobic digester* → *Biogas* → *Heat and power*

Elephant dung paper

A company in Thailand makes paper products from elephant dung. As the dung is mainly fibre, it is an excellent material for papermaking. A single elephant produces around 50 kg (110 lbs.) of dung a day, which can make about 115 sheets of paper.

Eat up, I've run out of paper!

Flying squirrel dung tea is used in Chinese medicine to cure stomach pain.

Disgusting data

During the 18th century, tanners would use a blend of human urine and dog poo to make leather. They would knead this foul mixture into animal hides until they became soft and easy to shape.

What happens to poo?

P oo contains germs, some of which can damage our health. That's why it's very important that we dispose of it safely. In the developed world, most people have flushing toilets that wash our waste safely away. This is not always the case in the developing world; in some remote villages, people must go to the toilet in the open, and germs from their faeces can contaminate local water supplies. This can endanger the health of those who use the water, and also harm wildlife.

Always remember to wash your hands after going to the toilet.

Sewage treatment

After poo has been flushed, it is carried through pipes to a sewage treatment plant. Here, it is filtered and treated to clean it of impurities. Purified liquid waste is released into waterways. The remaining solid waste (sludge) is dumped, or dried and sold to farmers as fertiliser.

Bye-bye!

How does nature deal with poo?

Time to start a new island.

In nature, poo often benefits the environment. For example, sea cucumbers excrete a mineral used to build coral reefs. Worm poo helps fertilise the soil. And parrot fish excrete sand. After thousands of years, this forms the white sandy beaches of Caribbean islands.

Spreading seeds

The tambaqui fish of the Amazon help to disperse tree seeds in the rain forest. The fish eat the seeds that fall from the trees, then excrete them so they can sprout somewhere else.

The trees feed me, so I do my bit to help them!

Animal poo can be dangerous. Dog and cat poo can cause diseases in humans if not disposed of safely. And cow dung pollutes the atmosphere and waterways.

Fascinating fact

The average person:
- excretes almost a tonne of poo a year
- visits the toilet 2,500 times a year
- spends about 3 years of his or her life on the toilet

Glossary

Allergic reaction A damaging response by the body to a substance.

Anaerobic digester A tank in which bacteria break down organic matter in the absence of oxygen.

Anus The opening at the end of the digestive tract through which poo leaves the body.

Artery Any of the tubes that carry blood from the heart to the other parts of the body.

Bacteria Microscopic organisms, some of which can cause disease.

Biogas A gaseous fuel such as methane, produced by the breakdown of organic matter in the absence of oxygen.

Biomethane A purified form of biogas that can be used as natural gas.

Carbohydrate A substance found in foods such as potatoes, pasta and sugar, that gives the body energy.

Conservationist Someone who helps preserve wildlife and the environment.

Dehydration A state in which a person has lost a large amount of water.

Excrete Expel waste.

Faeces Waste matter discharged from the intestines after food has been digested. Another word for poo.

Fibre A substance found in foods such as cereals, which resists digestion and helps move digested food through the intestines.

Gastric juices Acidic fluids produced by the stomach for digesting food.

Global warming A gradual increase in the temperature of the Earth's atmosphere caused by increased levels of carbon dioxide and other pollutants.

Guano Bird and bat poo.

Intestine The lower part of the digestive system, from the end of the stomach to the anus.

Larva The immature form of an insect.

Manure Animal dung used as fertiliser.

Minerals Substances such as iron and calcium needed by the body for good health.

Mucus A slimy substance produced by the body for protection and lubrication.

Nutrient A substance that provides nourishment needed for growth and a healthy life.

Oesophagus The tube connecting the throat to the stomach.

Protein A type of chemical essential to all living organisms.

Rectum The final section of the large intestine, ending at the anus.

Salivary glands Organs inside the cheeks and under the tongue that secrete saliva into the mouth.

Sewage Solid and liquid waste carried in sewers.

Stool Another word for poo.

Vegan A person who doesn't eat or use animal products.

Vein Any of the tubes in the body that carry blood towards the heart.

Virus A tiny organism that can reproduce and grow only when inside living cells. Viruses cause diseases such as the common cold and gastroenteritis (stomach flu).

Vitamins Substances that are essential for normal growth and nutrition. We need to include them in our diet because they cannot be produced by the body.

Index